# Contents

## Chapter 1

## The cub

While his eyes were still closed, the little cub knew his mother, who gave him food, warmth and love. Deep inside the cave, he snuggled close to her and dozed.

When his eyes opened, the first thing he saw was the light at the mouth of the cave. It drew him to it. He was always crawling and sprawling towards the edge of the cave, and his mother was always nudging him back with her nose.

One day, when his mother was out hunting, he crawled right up to the dazzling wall of light.

He crept to the edge of the cave and looked out and saw the world. It was so bright, he was terrified and he crouched down. He gazed around, until he forgot he was scared, and he stepped out boldly into the air...

...and yelped loudly as he rolled all the way to the bottom of a long bumpy slope.

When he finally came to a stop, he sat up. He licked the mud off himself and looked around, as might the first man from Earth when he landed on Mars.

He began to move, clumsily, running into twigs, falling over logs and stubbing his toes and nose on rocks and branches. Before long, he tripped and fell into a bird's nest.

There were seven chicks in it, and at first the cub was scared of them. But they smelled good. He picked one up and put it in his mouth. It was delicious meat, and he didn't stop until he had eaten all seven.

He was just licking his lips when a feathered whirlwind bowled him over. It was the furious mother of the chicks, who pecked and pecked at him until he turned and fled.

The cub ran and ran, until he came to
a clearing and lay down. He was tired.
Suddenly, more than anything in the
world, he wished for his mother. So he
started to look for the cave, feeling lonely
and helpless and lost.

He had stumbled a few paces when a
strange creature with flashing yellow eyes
appeared: a weasel!

With a cry, the weasel rushed at him. He felt teeth sink into his throat. Snarling, the cub scrambled back, but the weasel held on and the snarl became a whimper.

The little cub would have died but, at that moment, his mother came bounding up. The weasel let go of the cub and leaped at the she-wolf. With one flick of her head, the she-wolf flung the weasel into the air and caught it in her jaws.

She nuzzled her cub and licked his cuts, as happy to find him as he was to be found. After eating the weasel together, they trotted home to their cave.

Soon after that, the cub began to go out hunting with his mother. He knew the law now: eat or be eaten. So he ate creatures that flew into the air, or ran away, or faced and fought him. Running and hunting made him happy. And, after he hunted, he lazed in the sunshine with a full belly. He was alive, excited and very proud of himself.

## Chapter 2

# The camp

One day, as he was trotting through the forest, the cub saw and smelled five live things that he had never seen before. He wanted to run away, but he was so scared he froze.

Five men sat around a fire, although the cub didn't know they *were* men – or what fire was. One of them stooped over him, and the cub bristled, baring his little fangs.

"Look! The white fangs!" the man said, laughing. He reached down to pick up the cub, and the cub bit his hand.

The next moment the cub was knocked over by a sharp blow. He sat up and cried loudly. He waited for his brave mother to dash in and save him.

His mother did come bounding up, snarling fiercely, but the cub was astonished by what happened next.

"Kiche!" one of the men cried out in surprise, "Kiche!"

The little cub saw his proud mother sink to the ground, whimpering and wagging her tail.

"It's been a year since she ran away, Gray Beaver," a man said, quickly slipping a tether around her neck.

"Her father was dog, and her mother was wolf," Gray Beaver replied. "But this little cub is nearly all wolf. His fangs are white, so White Fang will be his name. He will be my dog. I have spoken."

So the cub had a new home – the camp in the forest. He didn't like it. His mother was tied to a stick all day, and there were other dogs at the camp that rushed at him and scared him.

Still, he was amazed by the powerful men and their strange, colossal teepees, and by every new thing he discovered.

One day, he watched Gray Beaver rubbing two sticks together.

Something bright rose from the sticks, twisting and turning. White Fang crawled towards the flame and slowly put out his tongue.

He jumped back, and burst out in an explosion of howls and cries. The pain hurt more than anything he had ever known. While he cried and cried, the men burst out laughing.

White Fang understood that the men were laughing at him, and the laughter hurt him most of all. So he fled to his mother, the one creature in the world who was not laughing at him.

White Fang's mother was always there to protect him. But there was one thing she could not save him from: Lip-lip.

Lip-lip was a puppy like White Fang, but he was older, and he was a bully. He picked on White Fang whenever he strayed from his mother's side.

White Fang had no friends – Lip-lip made sure of that. He never played like a puppy – Lip-lip would not allow it. Soon, he got all the dogs to attack White Fang.

So White Fang became crafty, swift and cruel. He became as agile as a cat. He learned to fight all the dogs at once: he had to, or he would not have survived.

Then, one dreadful day, his mother was taken away, down the river in a canoe.

That night, White Fang howled and howled. He howled so much that Gray Beaver woke up and hit him.

When he was old enough,
White Fang started to pull a sled
with seven other dogs. He was the
leader of the team – and this made the
other dogs hate him even more.

All the other dogs saw all day was his
waving brush of a tail and his hind legs
fleeing away, and it made them long to
attack him.

Each night, when they were out of the harness, they sprang on him. White Fang had to fight them off with vicious snarls and bites.

"There's never been another one like White Fang," Gray Beaver said. "Never one so hated by his own kind, or so strong. I prize him more every day."

# Chapter 3

# Beauty

That summer, Gray Beaver took White Fang on a journey. It was the summer of 1898, and thousands of gold hunters were going up the Yukon river to try their luck. Gray Beaver stayed in Fort Yukon, selling bales of furs and mittens to the gold hunters. He made a fortune overnight.

Soon White Fang saw his first white men. They were strange looking, but their dogs didn't amount to much. The dogs were afraid of him. They could sense that White Fang was from the wild.

White Fang and a gang of other dogs enjoyed wreaking havoc among the white men's dogs, and the men in Fort Yukon enjoyed watching. One man always watched White Fang and cheered him on. He was called Beauty by the other men, although he was anything but a beauty. He had dirty yellow eyes, dirty yellow teeth and dirty yellow hair, and he was known as the greatest coward in the country.

"How much for your dog?" Beauty asked Gray Beaver.

"I won't sell him, not for any price," Gray Beaver replied. "He's the strongest sled dog I have."

But the next week, Beauty Smith came back with a black bottle of whisky for Gray Beaver. Every week or so he brought another bottle. Before long, Gray Beaver wanted more and more whisky and his money began to run out. The shorter his money was, the shorter his temper. The next time Beauty visited him, his goods, his money and his temper were all gone.

"I could pay you for that dog in whisky," Beauty said, his lip curling with excitement.

"You catch the wolf, you can keep him," Gray Beaver replied.

"I'll bring the bottle, you catch him," Beauty said.

The next time White Fang came back to camp, Gray Beaver slung a noose around his neck and handed the end to Beauty Smith. White Fang's hair rose on end. He bared his teeth. He could sense that Beauty was cruel.

As Beauty started to lead him away, White Fang hurled himself at him, but Beauty was ready and knocked White Fang to the ground.

White Fang crawled limply to his feet, and followed Beauty Smith, his tail between his legs.

At home, Beauty tied him up and went to bed. Once he was asleep, White Fang bit through the rope in seconds, and trotted happily back to his master.

The next day, Gray Beaver took him straight back to Beauty, and White Fang got a terrible beating. That night, he ran home to Gray Beaver again.

When Gray Beaver handed him over for the third time, Beauty beat him to within an inch of his life. At first he couldn't stand up, and Beauty had to wait for an hour before they could head off. Sick, blind and reeling, White Fang followed Beauty home. This time, he was tied with a chain.

# Chapter 4

## The fighting wolf

Beauty Smith kept White Fang in a small pen. He loved to tease and torture him. He soon discovered that White Fang hated being laughed at and so he laughed at him all the time.

In that pen, White Fang became more savage than ever. He hated the chain that bound him, the men that laughed at him, and the dogs that came and snarled at him. Most of all, he hated Beauty Smith.

There was a reason why Beauty Smith was making White Fang so angry. One day, he brought a crowd of men to the pen. Beauty entered, club in hand, and slipped the chain from White Fang's neck.

Then a huge dog – a mastiff – was thrust into the pen. White Fang had never seen a dog like it. But now, at last, he could unleash all his hatred. He leaped in with a flash of fangs that ripped the dog's neck. The dog plunged at White Fang, but White Fang was here, there and everywhere, jumping up and escaping him.

"Come on White Fang!" Beauty roared.

In the end, the mastiff was dragged out by its owner. White Fang had won. The men paid their bets to each other, and coins clinked in Beauty Smith's hand.

Beauty Smith quickly brought more dogs to fight White Fang. He never lost his footing, and he had a lightning quickness.

He won every fight, and every fight was a fight to the death. Before long, White Fang was known far and wide as the *Fighting Wolf*.

That autumn, Beauty Smith took White Fang north on the steamboat, and people paid money to look at him and poke sticks through the bars of his cage.

When he wasn't being prodded and stared at, White Fang fought. He fought dogs, wolves, and once a full grown lynx. Then there were no more animals strong enough to fight him, until a man came to town with a bulldog. For a week, the promised fight was the talk of the town.

# Chapter 5

# To the death

Beauty Smith slipped the chain from White Fang's neck and stepped back. For once, White Fang did not attack. He stood still, his ears pricked up.

"Come on Cherokee," someone shouted.

"Come on White Fang!" Beauty yelled.

The bulldog's owner pushed him into the ring, and he growled.

White Fang's hair stood up on end. He had never seen a dog like this. But with a catlike swiftness he slashed with his fangs at the bulldog's ear.

Cherokee followed after White Fang, but White Fang sprang in again, slashed again, and got away untouched.

Still, his strange enemy only followed him slowly around the ring. White Fang danced and dodged, leaping in and out, biting the bulldog.

The bulldog just followed him slowly. Sooner or later he would get his teeth around White Fang's neck, and then he would win the battle.

"Do it Cherokee!" the men shouted. "Come on Cherokee!"

White Fang rushed again at Cherokee. This time he hit him so hard he was thrown into the air. For the first time in his fighting life he lost his footing. He fell onto his side – and Cherokee's teeth closed on his throat.

White Fang sprang to his feet and tore wildly around, trying to shake off the bulldog. Around and around he went, barking madly and trying to shake off the great weight. But Cherokee shut his eyes and held on.

The bulldog was slowly throttling White Fang. He fell to his side and lay still, panting for breath. It looked as if the battle was over.

Then Beauty Smith began to laugh, and White Fang went wild with rage. He got to his feet and stumbled madly around. But Cherokee still held on.

"Cherokee! Cherokee!" shouted the crowd, and Cherokee thumped his tail.

When Beauty saw White Fang's eyes
begin to close, something snapped inside
him. He jumped into the ring, and began
to kick him savagely. Just then, a stranger
jumped out of the crowd.

"You coward! You beast!" he shouted,
landing Beauty with a punch. Beauty
Smith lurched at him, so he punched him
again, and Beauty fell back.

"Come on Matt, lend a hand," he called to his friend, and the two men jumped into the ring to help White Fang.

They tried to loosen the dogs, but the bulldog's jaws were locked on White Fang's throat.

"Beasts!" he said to the onlookers. "Won't at least some of you help?"

But the crowd only cheered him sarcastically. Still, he got his revolver between the jaws of the bulldog, and slowly pried them apart. Very slowly, he managed to pull White Fang's mangled neck free.

As Cherokee was dragged away, White Fang sank down into the snow. His eyes were half closed, and he looked as if he had been strangled to death.

"He's just about all in," Matt said, "but he's breathin' all right."

Beauty Smith was on his feet again.

"Say, how much is a dog worth, all mangled like that?" the stranger asked.

"About a hundred and fifty dollars," someone called.

"Then that's what I'm going to give you for him," the stranger told Beauty.

Beauty Smith put his hands behind his back. "I ain't a-selling," he said.

"Oh yes you are," the man replied. "Because I'm buying. Here's your money. The dog's mine."

"I'm a man, I've got my rights."

"You're not a man, you're a beast," the man spat at Beauty. "Do you want the money, or do I have to hit you again?"

"I'll have the law on you," Beauty said.

"If you open your mouth, I'll hound you out of town. Understand?"

"Yes," Beauty muttered.

"Yes what?"

"Yes, sir," Beauty snarled.

"Who *is* he?" a man in the crowd whispered.

"Weedon Scott," someone answered. "A mining expert. He's in with all the big wigs. If you want to keep out of trouble, you'll steer clear of him."

So Beauty Smith stumbled away, cursing to himself, and Weedon Scott took White Fang home.

# Chapter 6

# A new life

"It's hopeless," Weedon confessed. He and Matt were looking out of their cabin at White Fang. Matt shrugged. Together they watched White Fang on the end of his tether, snarling and bristling.

"He's a wolf and there's no taming him," Weedon said. "We've had him two weeks, and he's wilder than he's ever been. What can I do?"

"Turn him loose," Matt said, "and take a club with you."

So Weedon went over to White Fang, and loosed the rope from around his neck. White Fang could hardly believe it. Since he had belonged to Beauty, he had not known a single moment of freedom.

"There, there," Weedon said soothingly, "I'm not gonna hurt you."

But White Fang was suspicious. *Something* was going to happen. He bristled and showed his teeth. The man's hand came out and touched his head.

White Fang snarled menacingly and sank low to the ground. But the hand stayed on his head. White Fang sprang up.

"Argh!" Weedon clutched his torn, bloody hand.

White Fang crouched down and backed away. He knew now he'd get a beating as bad as any from Beauty Smith.

"What are you doing?" Scott shouted.

Matt had dashed into the cabin and returned with a rifle.

"I reckon I should kill 'im," said Matt.

White Fang had jumped up and was now snarling with blood-curdling viciousness at Matt. The two men stared at him. Wherever the rifle pointed, White Fang leaped away from it.

"Well look at that," Matt said. "That dog is just too intelligent to shoot."

White Fang waited for his punishment: he knew it was coming now. With his hand bandaged, Weedon walked up to him and sat down a short distance away. He had no club in his hand.

Weedon began to talk and the hair rose on White Fang's neck. He growled.

But Weedon talked to White Fang as he had never been talked to before – soothingly and gently. In spite of himself, White Fang began to be less afraid.

After a long time, Weedon stood up and went into the cabin. White Fang expected him to return with a gun, but he came back with a small piece of meat and tossed it onto the snow. White Fang's body was tense – ready to spring away from a blow. He pricked up his ears and looked at it suspiciously. There was no telling what cruelty lay behind the piece of meat.

White Fang sniffed it, keeping his eyes on the man. It smelled good. He swallowed it. It tasted good too.

He was thrown more and more pieces, and he ate them up. Finally the man refused to toss the meat. Instead he held it out with his hand. With his ears flattened back, White Fang growled as he crept forward, took the meat from the hand... and nothing happened.

He ate more meat, and still there was no punishment. But now the hand came down to hurt him. White Fang shrank down under the hand. He growled, snarled and bristled and flattened his ears. He was ready to spring up when the blow struck.

But the blow didn't come. A hand came down on his head, and lifted up again.

White Fang knew some punishment was coming. He longed to flee, or spring up. But at the same time, the voice soothed him. His master talked softly, and his hand rose and fell.

Although everything in him longed to run, White Fang stayed still. It was the end of an old life for White Fang. A new, much, fairer life was beginning.

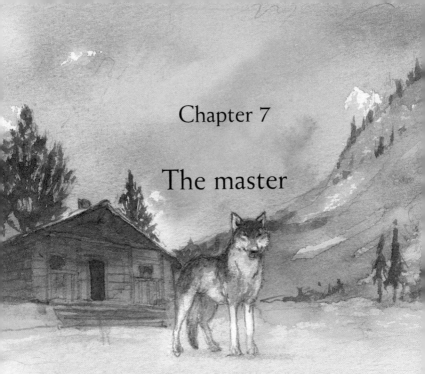

# Chapter 7

# The master

Every day, Weedon patted White Fang. And, day by day, White Fang got used to being patted. At first he put up with it, but later, he even came to enjoy it.

He was too set in his ways to ever bark a welcome to his new master, or bound up to greet him. But he pulled his master's sled, and he guarded his house faithfully each night. Day by day, he grew more fond of him, although he didn't show it.

In the spring, Weedon went away on business. A few weeks later, he received a note from Matt.

Weedon
The wolf won't work. Won't eat.
He wants to know what has become of you,
and I don't know how to tell him.
Think he might die.
Matt

It was true. In the cabin, White Fang lay on the floor, with no interest in food, in Matt, or in life. Matt might talk gently to him or swear at him, but it was all the same. He never did more than turn his dull eyes upon Matt, then drop his head on his forepaws.

Late one night, Matt was startled by a low whine from White Fang. He was up on his feet, his ears cocked towards the door, and he was listening intently.

A moment later, Matt heard a footstep. The door opened, and Weedon Scott stepped in. The two men shook hands.

"Holy smoke!" Matt exclaimed. "Look at him wag his tail!"

Weedon Scott strode across the room and White Fang came to him and gazed up at him, light shining in his eyes.

"He never looked at me that way, all the time you were gone!" Matt said.

Weedon squatted down and petted White Fang. He rubbed at the roots of his ears, stroked his neck, and tapped his spine gently with the tips of his fingers.

White Fang growled affectionately, and then, quite suddenly, he nudged his way in between his master's arm and body, and snuggled there.

The two men looked at each other.
Weedon's eyes were shining.

"Gosh!" said Matt. "I always insisted
that wolf was a dog. Look at him!"

White Fang was better in two days. And
having learned to snuggle, he did it often.

One night, Weedon and Matt sat playing cards when there was a loud cry and the sound of snarling outside the house. They jumped to their feet.

"The wolf's got somebody," Matt said.

"Bring a light!" Weedon shouted as he ran outside. Matt ran out after him with the lamp.

In the lamplight, they saw a man lying on his back in the snow, trying to fight off White Fang.

The next instant Weedon had White Fang by the throat and was dragging him clear, while Matt helped the man to his feet. He gasped and let go when he saw who it was.

Beauty Smith stood blinking in the lamplight. Matt looked down and saw two objects lying in the snow, a steel dog-chain and a stout club. Matt spun Beauty around and sent him into the darkness.

"Tried to steal you, eh?" Weedon said. "And you wouldn't have it. Well, he made a mistake, didn't he?"

"Must have thought he was fighting seventeen devils," Matt said, smirking.

That night, White Fang kept snarling, long after Beauty Smith was gone.

# Chapter 8

# A broken window

Something was in the air. White Fang sensed that something terrible was about to happen, even before there was any evidence for it. He lay down on the floor and gave a low, sad whine.

"That dog's on to you," Matt said. "He knows you're leaving him."

"Well, what the devil can I do with a dog in California?" Weedon replied. "He'd kill all the dogs he met on sight. The police would take him away and put him down. No, it would never do."

"You're right," Matt said. Then, after a pause, he added: "Still, there's no denying he thinks a lot of you."

"I know my mind – and what's best!" Weedon snapped.

The next day, White Fang spied his master packing his bags through the open cabin door. That night, he lifted his muzzle to the stars and let out a long, lonely wolf howl.

Inside the cabin, the two men were getting ready for bed.

"Listen to that, will you?" Matt said. "I wouldn't be surprised if he dies this time around."

Weedon's blankets rustled. "Oh be quiet and stop going on about it!"

The next day Weedon was going to California for good. "Give me one last goodbye growl, won't you?" he said to White Fang. But White Fang refused.

Just then the steamship hooted on the river. The two men set off down the hill.

"Take good care of him, Matt," Weedon said. Inside the house, White Fang had begun to howl as if his master had died.

When Weedon and Matt got to the steamship, it was jammed with people. And there, sitting on the deck, was White Fang. The two men stared at him in shock.

"You locked the doors?" Weedon asked.

"You bet I did."

"Look, there are cuts on his muzzle," Weedon said. "He must have leaped clean through the window!"

"I'll take him ashore," Matt said.

The boat's whistle hooted. Weedon had to think quickly. He shook Matt's hand.

"You've no need to worry about taking care of the wolf," he said.

"What? You don't mean it?"

"I do," Weedon said. A minute later Matt stood on the shore as the ship set off down the river.

"He won't like the climate!" Matt shouted. "Just make sure you clip his hair in the summer!"

Weedon bent over the wolf standing beside him, patted his head and rubbed his ears. "Now growl," he said.

# Chapter 9

# The sleeping wolf

When the steamer arrived in San Francisco, White Fang was terrified. Cable cars hooted and clanged and screeched down the streets. There was so much noise! There were so many men! White Fang felt small, helpless and dizzy – but it was all over as quickly as a bad dream.

He was put into a carriage, and soon it was driving up to a house. When White Fang jumped out, the countryside lay all around him.

There were lots of people to get used to at his new home. Weedon lived there with his wife, his young children and his parents.

Day by day, White Fang got used to the new people. He thought of them as precious possessions of his master, so he took great care of them.

He got used to the children petting him. And he liked sitting quietly beside Weedon's father on the porch as he read in the afternoon sun. The months came and went. White Fang grew fat, happy and content.

White Fang even got to like Collie, the sheepdog who lived there. One afternoon, she nipped at his shoulder playfully. She ran off into the forest and he followed her. They ran together, just like his mother and father had done, years before.

Around this time, the newspapers were full of the daring escape of a murderer from prison. His name was Jim Hall, and he was on his way to get his revenge on the man who had put him behind bars: Judge Scott – Weedon's father.

One night, while everyone was asleep, White Fang woke up. Lying in the hall, he sniffed the air, listened, and knew at once there was a stranger in the house. The stranger was moving softly, but White Fang followed silently behind him. He knew the advantage of surprise.

The stranger paused at the foot of the staircase. At the top of the staircase was his master and his possessions. White Fang bristled, and waited. The stranger lifted his foot – and White Fang struck. He jumped through the air and landed on the stranger, burying his fangs in his neck.

The house awoke to what sounded like a battle of devils downstairs. Shots were fired, a man screamed in horror – and the staircase was flooded with light.

In the middle of the floor, a dead man was lying.

"Jim Hall," Weedon Scott said grimly.

White Fang, too, was lying on the ground. His eyes were closed.

"He's all out," Weedon muttered.

"We'll see about that," Judge Scott replied, reaching for the telephone.

"Frankly, he has one chance in a thousand," the surgeon announced, looking down at White Fang. "Three broken ribs – one that's pierced his lungs. And three bullet holes clear through him."

"He mustn't lose any chance he has," Judge Scott said. "Spare no expense."

For three weeks, White Fang clung to life. He lay with his eyes closed, dreaming. He dreamed he was in the cave with his mother, or that Gray Beaver was looking down at him. Or he was back in Beauty Smith's pen, terrified. He whimpered as he dreamed of the city. At last, his bandages were taken off.

The whole family gathered to look as White Fang rose slowly to his feet. He fell down several times, but at last he stood on his four legs.

"He'll have to learn to walk again; he might as well start now," said the surgeon.

So White Fang tottered outside. Collie lay by the stables, with six pudgy puppies playing around her in the sun.

White Fang looked on, amazed. The master shoved one little puppy towards him. He looked at the puppy, sprawled in front of him. Then their noses touched, and he licked the puppy's tiny face.

Weedon and his family clapped, but White Fang was puzzled. He lay down and all the puppies came to him. He let them clamber and scramble and tumble over him, and then he lay, with half-shut eyes, drowsing in the sun.

# Jack London (1876-1916)

Jack London's life was as extraordinary as his stories. Born into a poor family in San Francisco, he went to work in a factory when he was only fourteen. At fifteen, he became a pirate, stealing oysters. At seventeen, he was a sailor and at eighteen, he was sent to prison for begging.

At the age of twenty-one, he joined the gold rush. Six years later, his first novel, *The Call of the Wild*, made him world famous. He moved to a ranch in Sonoma County, California, where he wrote many more books and short stories about people and animals.